Junior Science
trees

Terry Jennings

Illustrations by David Anstey

Gloucester Press
New York · London · Toronto · Sydney

About this book

You can learn many things about trees from this book. It tells you about the parts of a tree and what each part does. There are lots of activities and experiments for you to try. You will learn about different kinds of trees, how to measure a tree, how to press leaves and flowers, and much more.

First published in the United States in 1991 by Gloucester Press 387 Park Avenue South New York, NY 10016

© Mirabel Books Limited 1990

This book was designed and produced by Mirabel Books Limited

Printed in Belgium

Library of Congress Cataloging-in-Publication Data

Jennings, Terry J.
    Trees / Terry Jennings.
        p. cm. -- (Junior science)
    Includes index.
    Summary: An introduction to various types of trees, with emphasis on their basic parts.
    ISBN 0-531-17276-7
    1. Trees--Juvenile literature. [1. Trees.] I. Title. II. Series: Jennings, Terry J. Junior science.
    QK475.8.J46   1991
    582.16--dc20   90-44671   CIP   AC

leaves

twigs

branches

trunk

roots

A tree is a large plant with a thick woody stem, or trunk. It has deep roots and branches that carry twigs and leaves. The roots hold the tree in the ground and take up water and minerals from the soil.

Trees are too tall for you to measure their height directly. But here is a way you can do it. Get a friend to hold a yardstick under the tree you want to measure. Stand back and hold up a pencil. Move your thumb until the pencil looks the same length as the stick. Then see how many times the length of the pencil goes into the height of the tree. The tree in the picture is 33 feet tall. The tallest tree in the world is a redwood, or giant sequoia, tree in California. It is 364 feet tall. See which is the tallest tree you can find.

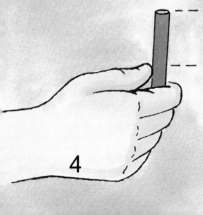

The distance around a tree's trunk is called its girth. You can measure it with a tape measure. See which tree has the largest girth. It may not also be the tallest.

5

maple

oak

ash

willow

All trees have leaves and they
come in all kinds of shapes and sizes.
Some leaves, such as maple leaves,
are wide. Pine needles are very narrow,
like needles. Leaves called compound leaves

sycamore

beech

pine

holly

are made up of many small leaflets. An ash
tree has compound leaves. Some leaves are
prickly like a holly leaf. Leaves take in sunlight.
The plant uses it to help make food for the tree.
If leaves get covered in dust, they cannot take
in sunlight and the trees may die.

7

You can make a collection of tree leaves. Put the fresh leaves on sheets of newspaper, and cover them with more newspaper. Put some heavy books on top. After a few days the leaves will be dry and flat. Tape them to sheets of paper and write the name of the tree below each leaf.

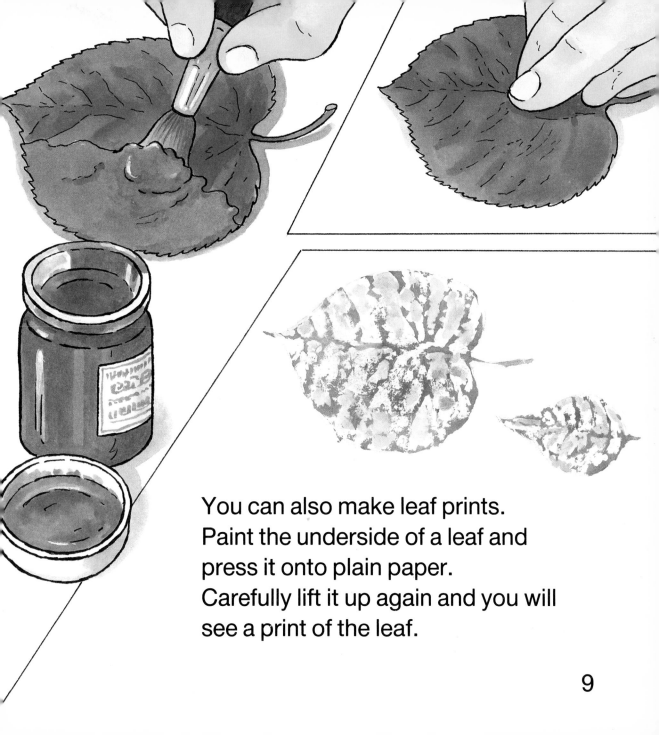

You can also make leaf prints.
Paint the underside of a leaf and
press it onto plain paper.
Carefully lift it up again and you will
see a print of the leaf.

9

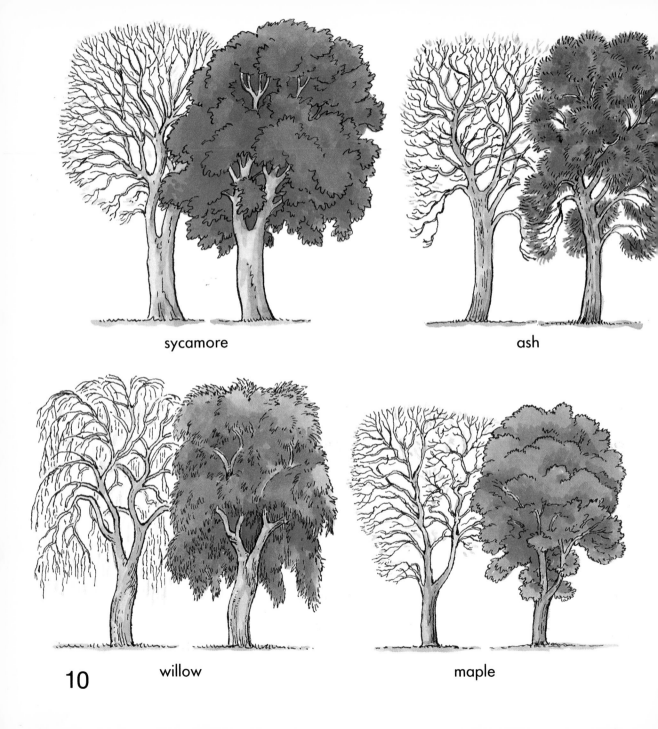

sycamore

ash

willow

maple

10

cedar   holly   pine

Trees that lose their leaves in winter are called deciduous trees. Oak and maple are deciduous; they grow new leaves each spring. Other trees lose only a few leaves at a time and then grow new ones. They keep their leaves in winter and are called evergreen trees. Pine and holly are evergreen trees. So are many of the trees that grow in tropical rainforests.

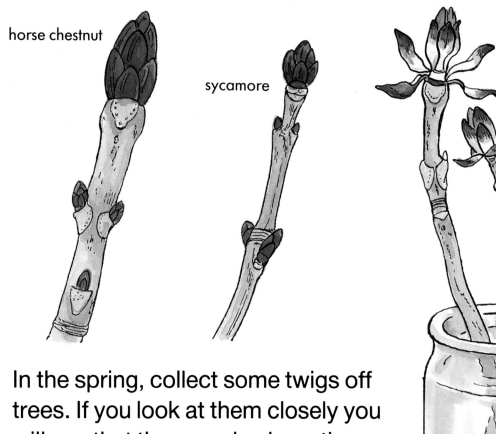

horse chestnut

sycamore

In the spring, collect some twigs off trees. If you look at them closely you will see that there are buds on the twigs. Put the twigs in a jar of water. You can keep a record of what happens by making a drawing of the twigs every few days. The buds will slowly open and tiny leaves will appear.

12

A tree trunk is covered with bark, which protects the tree. Some trees, such as oak trees, have rough bark; others, such as birches, have smooth bark

beech

pine

oak

birch

that peels off in layers. You can make a record of different kinds of bark by pinning a piece of paper to the bark of a tree and rubbing it with a wax crayon. The pattern of the bark will come out on the paper.

Beneath the bark of a tree is wood. Trees grow very slowly and each year a tree adds a new layer of wood to its trunk. You can see these layers by looking at the trunk of a tree that has been cut down. There is one layer for each year of growth.

By counting the layers you can figure out how old the tree is. We use wood for many things, from furniture to pencils. Even paper is made from wood. The book you are reading now was made from a tree.

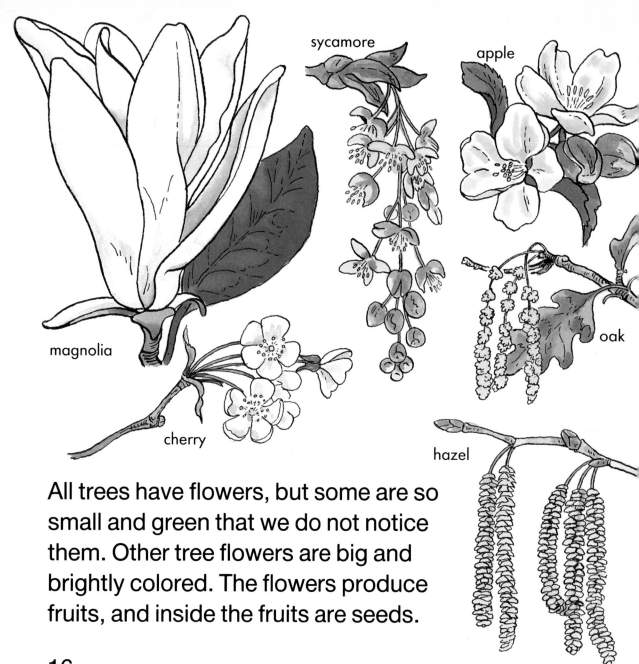

sycamore

apple

oak

magnolia

cherry

hazel

All trees have flowers, but some are so
small and green that we do not notice
them. Other tree flowers are big and
brightly colored. The flowers produce
fruits, and inside the fruits are seeds.

16

You can make a collection of tree flowers and press them between newspaper, like making a leaf collection. They make a good wallchart if you tape them to a sheet of cardboard and label them.

acorn

conker

ash

All trees grow from seeds. Even a big oak tree grows from a little acorn. Most trees make thousands of seeds each year, but only a few of them grow into trees. The seeds are scattered in various ways. Some are blown by the wind.

pine

apple

holly

18

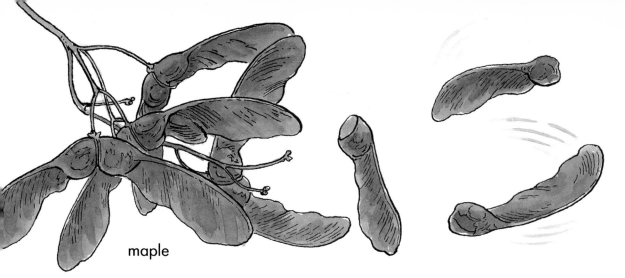

maple

Pine seeds and maple seeds are scattered in this
way. Other seeds are spread by birds and mammals.
The seeds of apple, oak and holly are scattered this
way. The birds and mammals eat some of the seeds,
but many get buried in the soil, where
they eventually grow into trees.

Most tree seeds stay in the soil all winter and do not start to grow until the spring. First a root grows down into the soil and then a shoot grows up toward the light. The shoot grows two leaves and a central bud, which in time produces more leaves. The roots spread out and slowly the seedling begins to look like a small tree. You can collect tree seeds and plant them in pots of soil. Or you can put large seeds on top of a jar or glass full of water.

oak seedli

Water the soil every week and keep the jar or glass full. Place them somewhere warm and light. After many weeks some of the seeds will begin to grow into seedlings.

oak seedling

Trees are among the most important plants. They give us wood and paper. They make part of the air we breathe. Many animals live and feed in trees.

You can make a book about your favorite tree. Draw pictures of it in the book. Draw it as it looks at different times of the year. Make pressings of leaves and flowers and tape or glue them in. Draw pictures of birds and other animals that you see in the tree.

glossary

Here are the meanings of some words that you might have met for the first time in reading this book.

bark: the outer covering of a tree trunk. It may be rough or smooth.

branch: part of a tree that sticks out from the trunk.

compound leaf: a leaf that is divided into several separate parts.

deciduous tree: a tree that loses its leaves in winter.

evergreen tree: a tree that has green leaves all the year through.

fruit: a part of a plant that contains the seeds.

root: the part of a plant that grows into the ground.

seed: a small part of a plant that can be sown in the ground to produce a new plant.

seedling: a very young plant.

trunk: the main stem of a tree.

twig: a thin part of a branch of a tree.

Index

PRINTED IN BELGIUM BY
proost
INTERNATIONAL BOOK PRODUCTION